BIG, BAD
BARNEY BEAR

BIG, BAD
BARNEY BEAR

Written and illustrated by
TONY ROSS

Andersen Press · London

Copyright ©1992 by Tony Ross
This paperback edition first published in 2002 by Andersen Press Ltd.
The rights of Tony Ross to be identified as the author and illustrator of this work
have been asserted by him in accordance with the Copyright, Designs and Patents Act, 1988.
First published in Great Britain in 1992 by Andersen Press Ltd, 20 Vauxhall Bridge Road, London SW1V 2SA.
Published in Australia by Random House Australia Pty., 20 Alfred Street, Milsons Point, Sydney, NSW 2061.
Copyright ©1992 by Tony Ross. Colour separated in Switzerland by Photolitho AG, Zurich.
Printed and bound in Italy by Grafiche AZ, Verona. All rights reserved.

10 9 8 7 6 5 4 3 2 1

British Library Cataloguing in Publication Data available.

ISBN 1 84270 058 8

This book has been printed on acid-free paper

Moose was bored, so he decided to go and find a job.

He found lots of work on the building site.

One shovel looked better than the others...

...so Moose chose it for himself.

Moose was not happy, but he started work.

He worked hard for an hour, until it was time for coffee.

Moose chose the cup that would hold the most coffee, but he had to take a smaller one.

Moose was not happy. He took his small cup of coffee and settled in a large comfy chair…

...but he had to move onto an uncomfortable pile of bricks.

Moose was not happy, he could take no more...

...and the other animals trembled.

The crocodile pointed to a factory that
BIG BAD BARNEY BEAR had built...

...but Moose was not impressed.
He wanted to find the bear...

...and put him in his place...

...once and for all!

At daybreak, Moose came across a lonely cottage, big enough
for a bear.

He knocked on the door, and it was opened by a huge animal.

With a roar, Moose charged. Skin and teeth flew, fur and
trouser buttons…

...until at last, Moose was the winner.

The bear was bruised, and baffled...

and didn't seem to understand...

...why.

More Andersen Press paperback picture books!

Scarecrow's Hat
by Ken Brown

Funny Fred
by Peta Coplans

Splosh!
by Philippe Corentin

Quack, Quack!
by Philippe Dupasquier

War and Peas
by Michael Foreman

Dilly Dally and the Nine Secrets
by Elizabeth MacDonald and Ken Brown

Princess Camomile Gets Her Way
by Hiawyn Oram and Susan Varley

Bear's Eggs
by Dieter and Ingrid Schubert

The Birthday Presents
by Paul Stewart and Chris Riddell

The Sand Horse
by Ann Turnbull and Michael Foreman

Frog and a Very Special Day
by Max Velthuijs

Dr. Xargle's Book of Earthlets
by Jeanne Willis and Tony Ross